THE EVENT

DANIEL GRANT   PART 1

NO ONE UNDER THE AGE OF CONSENT, IN WHATEVER JURISDICTION YOU HAPPEN TO FIND YOURSELF, SHOULD EVEN CONSIDER READING THIS COMIC. IF YOU DO, IT'S VERY LIKELY TO PERMANANTLY SHRIVEL YOUR SEX ORGANS.

YOU'VE BEEN WARNED.

THIS COMIC CONTAINS ALL THE GOOD STUFF, NUDITY, SEX AND VIOLENCE. IF ANY OF THE ABOVE CAUSE YOU ANGST --

PLEASE DO NOT READ ANY FURTHER.

ISBN-13: 978-1-948297-15-8

DALLENT

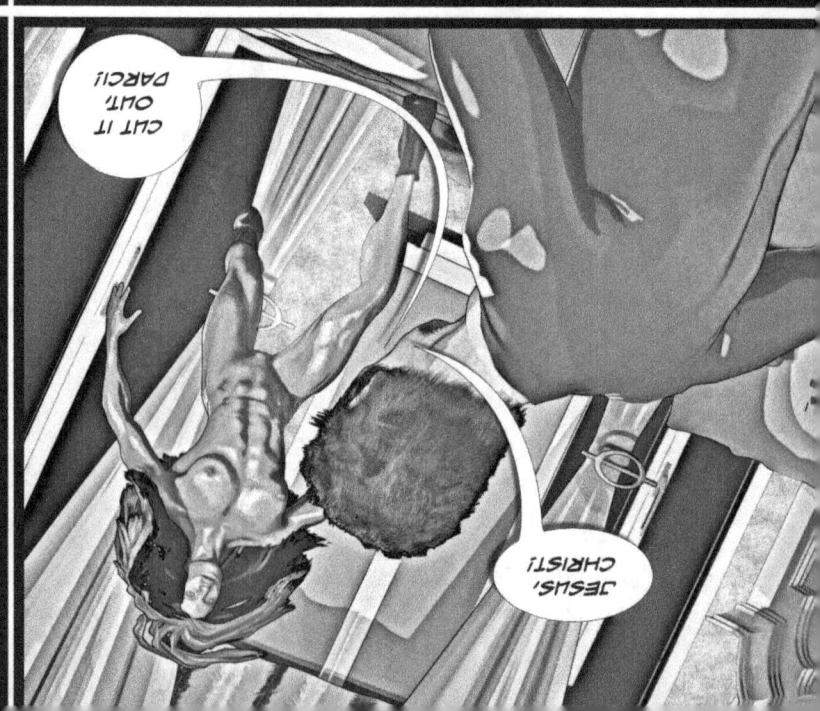

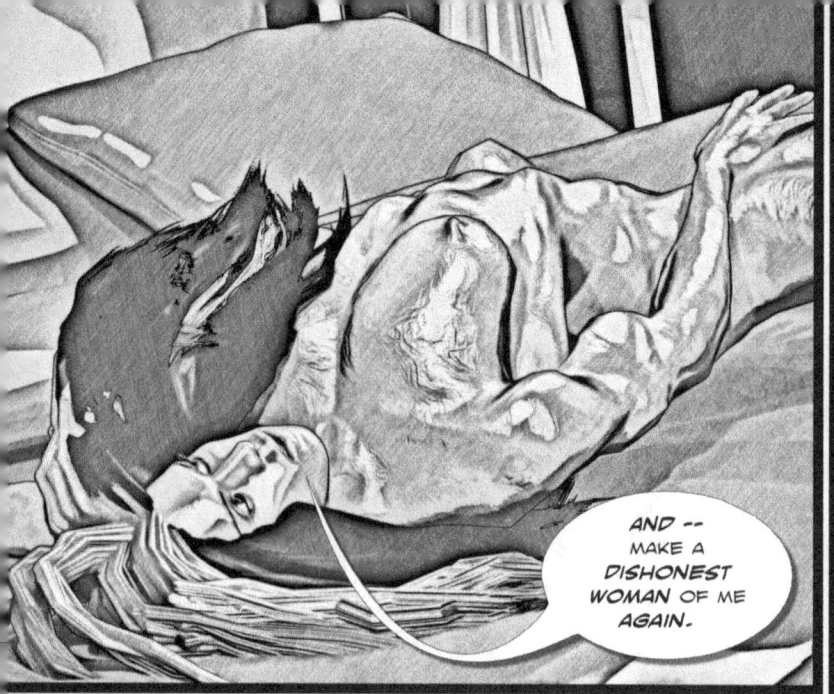

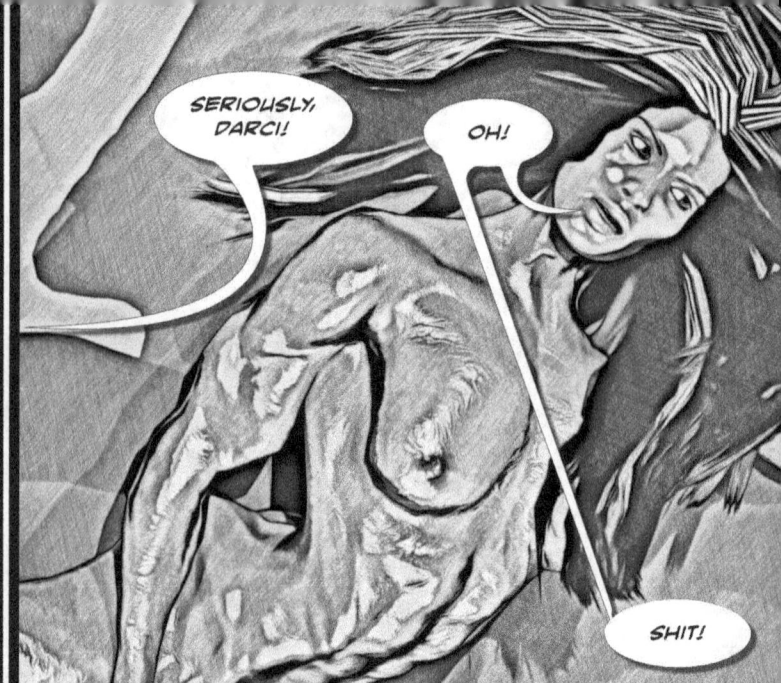

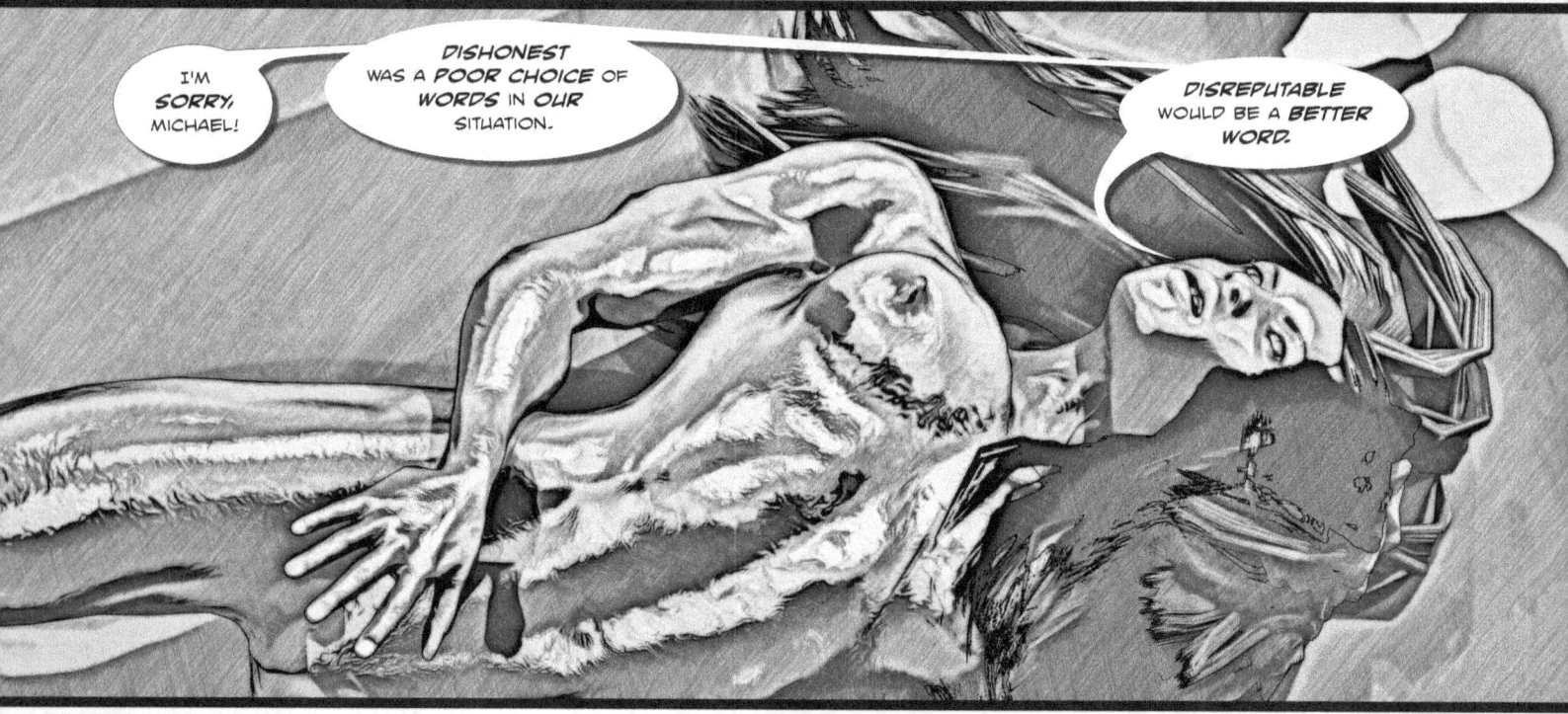

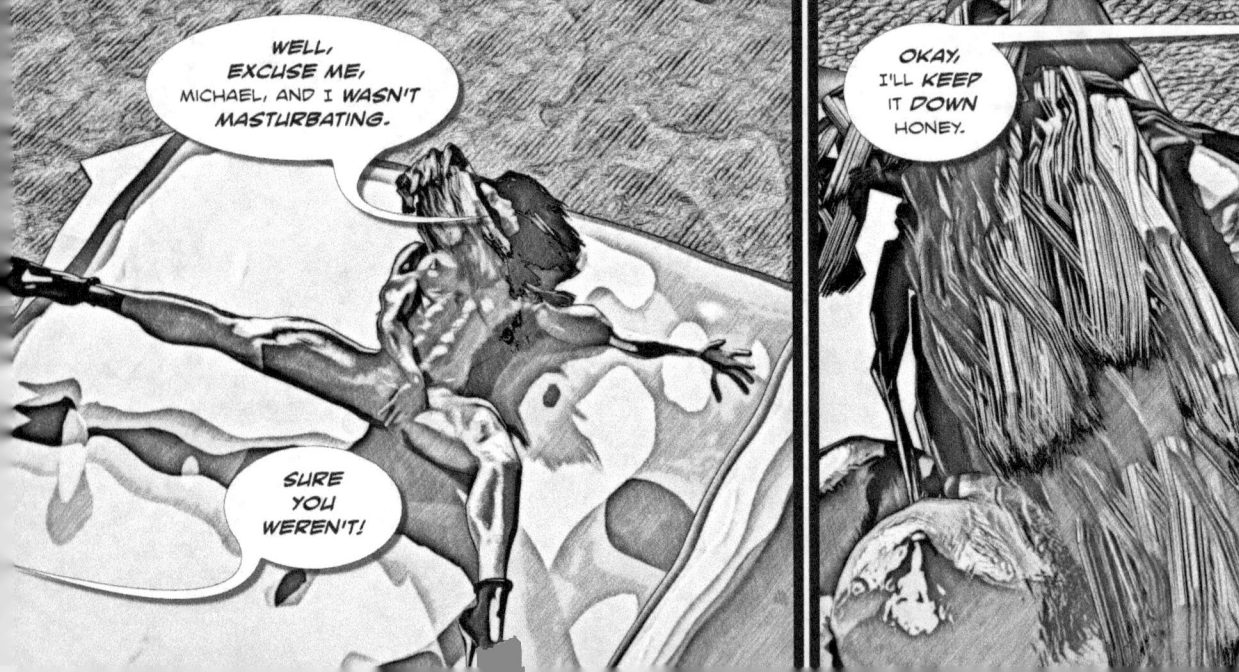

I'M **NOT** GOING TO **CHECK** YOUR **PHONE**, DARCI.

MY **COMMENT** WAS A **POOR** ATTEMPT AT **HUMOR**, NOTHING **MORE.**

OH, THANK, GOD!

AS FOR THE **JERKING** OFF, I'M A **HIGHLY SEXUAL** PERSON, MICHAEL . . .

HONEY, IT'S **JUST** GOING TO **TAKE** SOME **TIME!**

FINDING OUT ABOUT . . .

WELL . . .

YOU AND **HIM**, REALLY **ROCKED** ME!

I KNOW MICHAEL, AND I'M **REALLY** SORRY!

CAN I GET YOU **SOMETHING** BEFORE **WORK**, COFFEE, TEA, BACON AND EGGS . . .

ME -- **DRAPED** SUGGESTIVELY **OVER** THE OLE **BUTCHER'S** BLOCK.

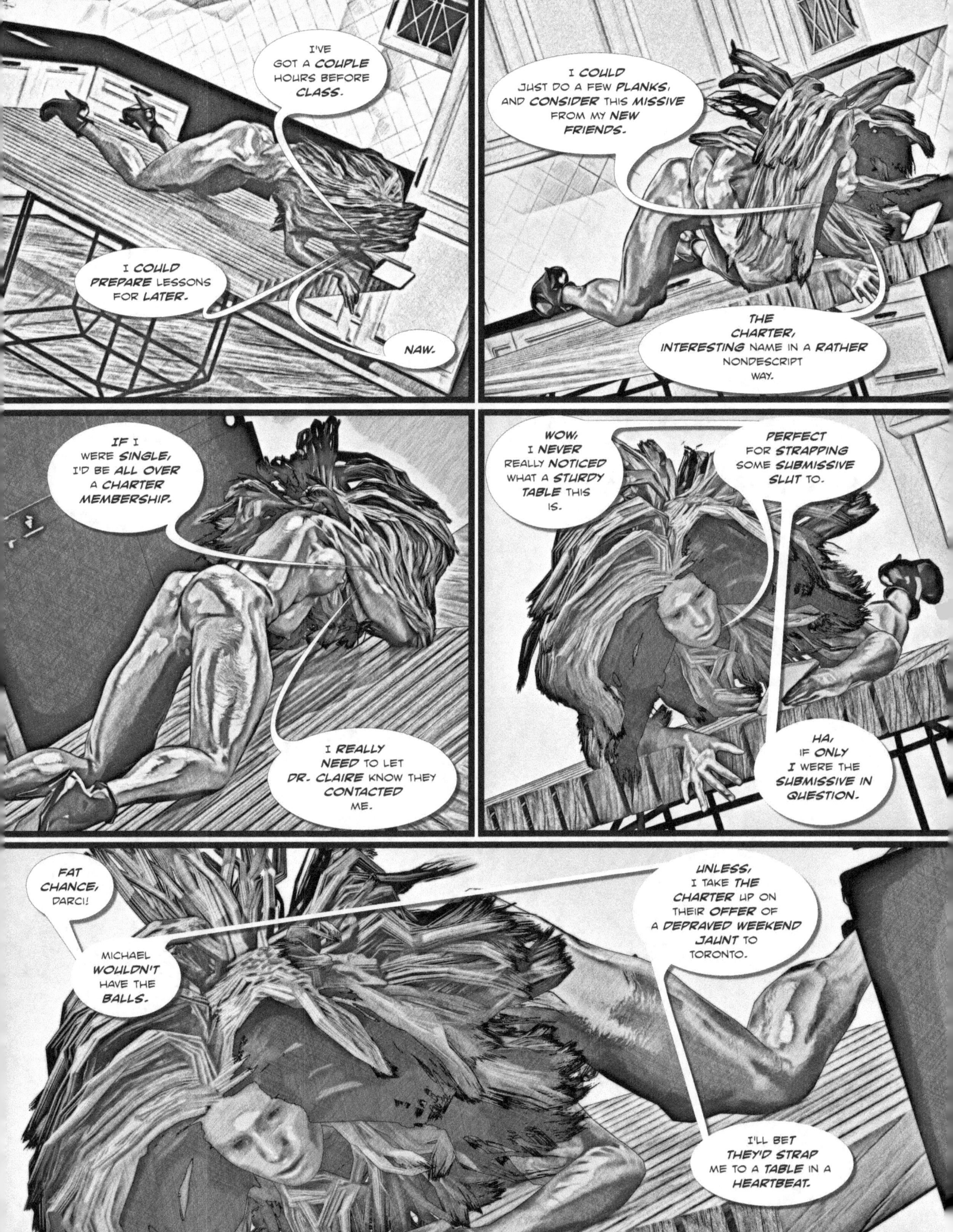

LATER THAT DAY.

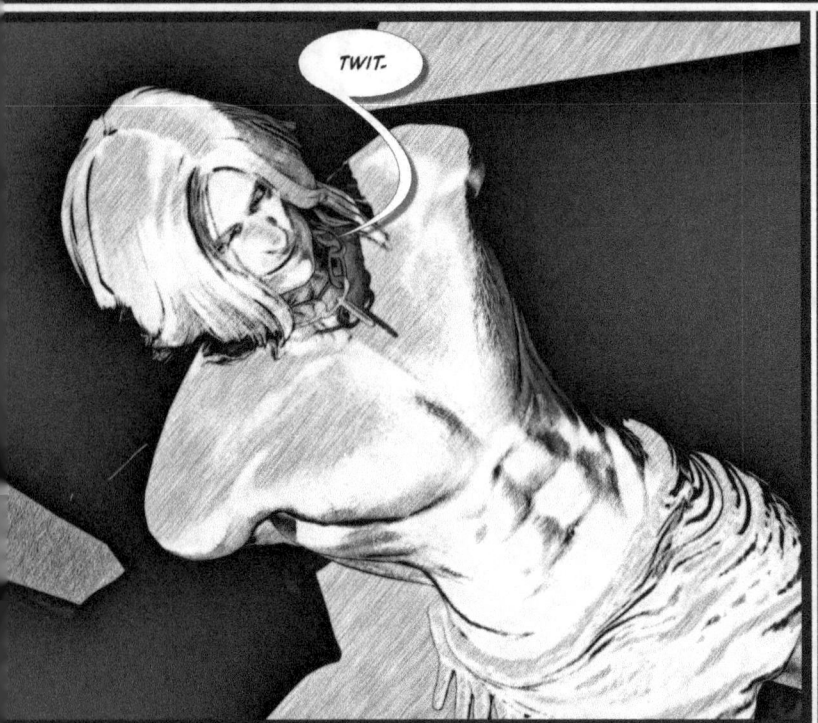

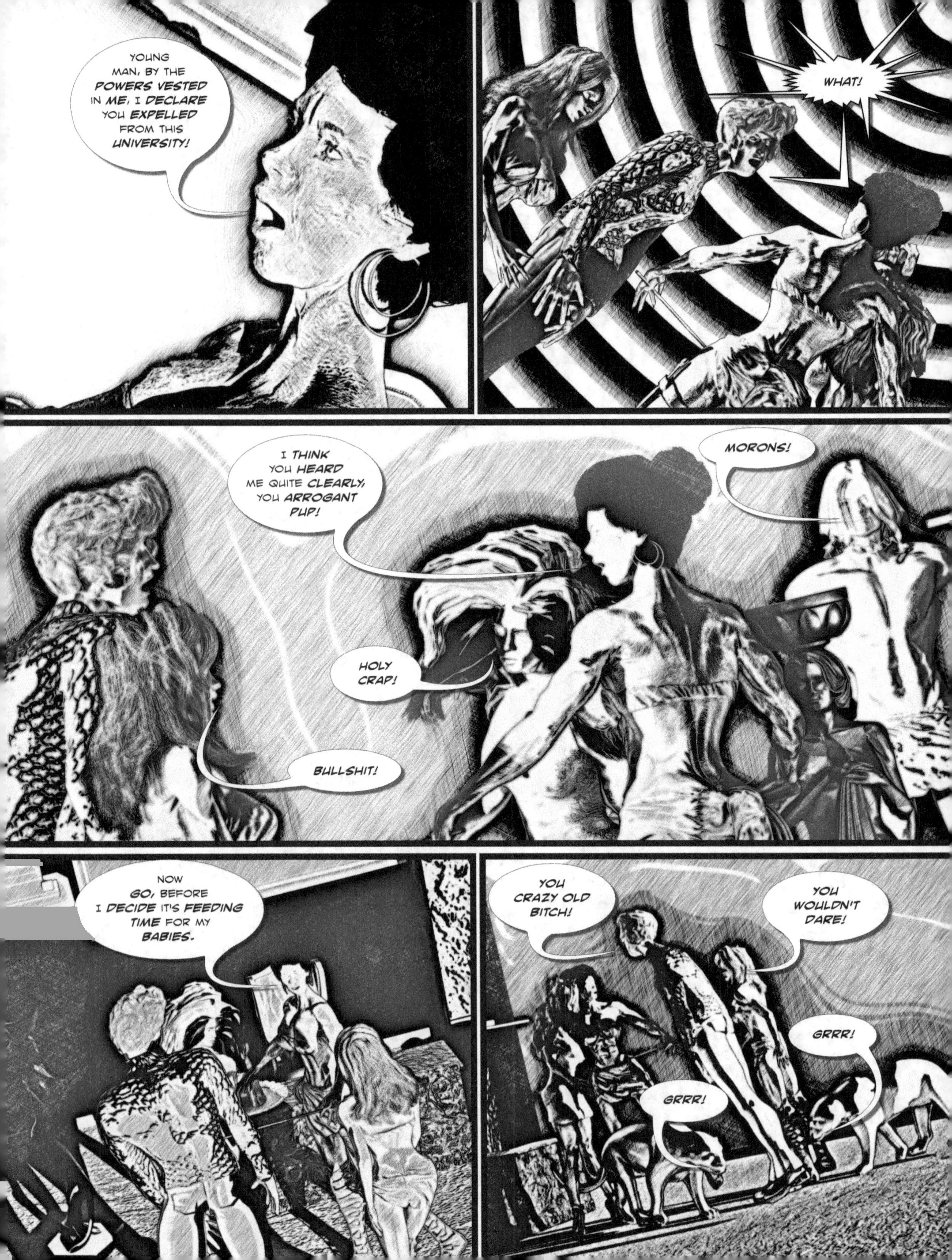